Cancer & the Lottery

Brinton Woodall

authorHOUSE®

AuthorHouse™
1663 Liberty Drive
Bloomington, IN 47403
www.authorhouse.com
Phone: 1 (800) 839-8640

Published by AuthorHouse 01/26/2015

ISBN: 978-1-4969-6425-0 (sc)
ISBN: 978-1-4969-6424-3 (e)

Library of Congress Control Number: 2015900657

Contents

Prologue

Marisa is a young Hispanic girl who is in her junior year of college. Marisa had a tough childhood. She had problems with the relationships that were vital in a child's life. She has a lot of emotional issues and does not know where to place the blame, whether on herself or on her mother. Marisa has a problem with allowing herself to live for the moment; she's used to having a plan for everything. She carries a book with her in she shares her most intricate thoughts and views.

Sarah is one of Marisa's friends. She is twenty-one and Caucasian, Sarah usually has a positive outlook on life. Sarah is joyful by nature and has a good sense of humor. Sarah and Marisa met during their freshman year of college.

Melinda is a twenty-one-year-old Hispanic who has Native American features: flawless skin and long black hair. Her personality represents a typical Taurus. She prefers peace, but if someone barks up the wrong tree, she is one of the nastiest women that have ever been seen walking on God's green earth. She also met Marisa in college.

Janice is African American and has been best friends with Marisa since the age of five. They both grew up in the same apartment building, and when Janice was eighteen years old, she moved in with Marisa. Janice has a big heart and is compassionate, especially when it comes to Marisa due to the problems Marisa dealt with as a child. Janice is Marisa's confidant and protector; they are more like sisters than they are friends.

Marisa

I've been having this headache. I hope my doctor appointment goes well and that Professor Morry will have us eventually stop documenting our lives in this journal. This class was supposed to be an easy A. It has turned out to be one of the deepest classes I have ever taken. Professor Morry is all about finding what you're destined to be. In our last class, Professor Morry asked us: If we could do three things to change our lives before we die, what would they be? The first thing I would do is travel and see parts of the world I have always dreamed of going to. If I could take one person to go with me, it would be Lisa. The second thing I want to do before I leave this earth is settle all my problems with my mom, and third, reunite with my sister. I hope I have more interesting things to write about, but this is a good start.

Marisa

The Classroom

Marisa is sitting in class listening to Professor Morry's lecture on the theory of having a bucket list. Sitting next to Marisa is Sarah and Melinda. Professor Morry is in his early fifties and Caucasian.

Professor Morry says, "OK, today I want to know what you think of dreams or goals. Does everyone get to complete their goals? Are we as humans afraid to reach our highest potential due to the fear of being completely submissive in faith? You can succeed or you can fail; there is not much in between. So to get back to my question, do all people that have the full capability of their minds make their dreams goals to be achieved in life?"

Marisa says, "If anything, we cut our dreams short."

Professor Morry says, "That is an interesting take. Can you explain?"

Marisa takes a deep breath to make sure she gets her point across. "Well, I think we need to ask ourselves: At what age do we start working toward our dreams? Think of your favorite artists or athletes. They work more than they dream. They envisioned success in their fields since they were kids. Most of us saw ourselves in college at a young age. That's a dream that most have had since we were young that seemed achievable, whether because our parents told us we could do it or because we knew it was a step that we could all take."

Professor Morry says, "The reason I ask about goals or dreams is because people don't have an idea of what they want to receive from the world. As humans, we are naive to think we will always have time, when the truth is that time is a man-made concept."

Professor Morry writes the assignment on the board in bold letters for everyone to see: If you were to die in a month, what would you want to accomplish or do? The students take a look at the board and leave the classroom. Professor Morry yells, "Take a chance and play the lottery!"

The Ticket

After class the girls walk toward the bodega. It is a beautiful fall day. The girls talk about what they have going on for the rest of the day.

Marisa, Jessica, and Melinda take some juice and a bag of chips to the register to buy along with their lottery numbers. A disgruntled Rico, the owner of the bodega, is running the cash register.

Rico says, "Come on, come on, let's go. Why you girls always take so long?"

Melinda says extremely fast with an accent, "Don't play with me, Rico. I'm feeling lucky-like today."

Rico rolls his eyes and asks all the girls for their lottery numbers. Marisa and Sarah tell Rico their numbers. Melinda continues to irk Rico. Sarah is pondering what number to pick as she looks to Marisa and Melinda for an idea; they just shrug their shoulders. Sarah just says the first group of numbers that comes to her head. "OK, my numbers are 55, 45, 28, 37, 18, and jackpot number is 17."

Marisa already knows what her numbers are going to be as she hands Rico a piece of paper with her numbers: 5, 19, 44, 33, 18, and jackpot number 22. Melinda gets her usual numbers and, after receiving her ticket, gives Rico her two cents.

"You so rude, Rico. You mad my aunt didn't give you none because you ugly."

Rico just points at the door as the girls leave the bodega and go their separate ways until they see each other tomorrow.

The Doctor Appointment

Marisa is not feeling well; she has constant migraines and can't feel certain parts of her body. Dr. Lehman asks her certain questions as he is testing her reflexes and notices she is not moving or flinching.

Marisa asks whether he knows what is causing her headache, but Dr. Lehman does not reply. He writes a prescription, as well as a referral for a CAT scan, slides his chair to the door, and hands the note to her with a forced smile.

The Winner is...

Janice is Marisa's roommate and is cleaning up the living room. Marisa walks in and greets Lisa.

Janice asks, "How was your appointment?"

"It was OK. I needed an extra test. I just came back from the pharmacy. What time do they show the lottery?"

"I think right now, actually."

"Can you change the channel real quick?"

Janice gives Marisa the remote so Marisa can change the channel to the news to watch the lottery. Marisa is watching the lottery very intently, listening to the numbers that are being said.

"Welcome to the eleven o'clock news, but let's get the jackpot number, which is worth one hundred fifty million dollars."

The news anchor continues, "And the first number is five." Marisa shakes her head to indicate she has that number as well.

"The next number is nineteen, then forty-four."

Janice is looking at Marisa and Marisa is looking back at Lisa. Marisa gets up to hear the rest of the numbers.

"Then we have thirty-three and eighteen, and the jackpot number is—"

Marisa screams, "Twenty-two! Please, twenty-two, come on, and come on!"

The news anchor says, "Twenty-two."

Marisa jumps up and runs all around the living room, screaming she has won, while Janice is in disbelief that Marisa has just won the lottery.

Marisa says, "Lisa, you can't tell anyone until I get the money. OK?"

"Marisa, how long you gonna have me wait before I can tell my mom?"

"I'm not even going to tell my mom. You have to promise me."

"I've known you since we were five years old. Pinkie promise, I won't tell anyone."

Marisa and Janice do a pinkie swear to keep Marisa's winnings on the hush. Janice is reluctant to commit to the pinky swear but eventually does, and they talk about the lottery until they both pass out in the living room with the television on.

The News

The next day, Marisa is in the waiting room, waiting to be called into the doctor's office to find out the results. She reads the community magazines to keep herself from going crazy waiting for her name to be called. She feels that everyone is looking at her, although this is all in her mind; she is paranoid due to winning the lottery.

The nurse calls for Marisa and escorts her to Dr. Lehman's office so Marisa and the doctor can talk about the results. Dr. Lehman walks in and takes a deep breath; he looks Marisa in the eye to the point where Marisa gets nervous and her hands start shaking.

"Dr. Lehman, what's wrong?"

"Marisa, there is no easy way to say this. So I am going to just come right out and say it. The CAT scan shows that you have an advanced inoperable brain tumor, and in our estimation, you have three weeks—if you're lucky, a month—to live."

Marisa starts to cry hysterically after hearing the news as she is distraught, knowing she just won the lottery and now all of this is happening.

Dr. Lehman tries to be as consoling as possible but does not have any words to say that can make the news any better. So Marisa gives Dr. Lehman a handshake and leaves his office after she dries her tears.

Marisa, devastated at what she has just found out, is now looking at a calendar, trying to predict the number of days she has left to live. This brings unnecessary anxiety into Marisa's life. Marisa opens up her notebook to confess the feelings of the day.

28 Days Left

Do I tell my friends I have a month to live? Do I tell my friends that I won the lottery? What is a month? Is that thirty-one days or exactly four weeks? Do I tell my mother? I haven't spoken to her since I was eighteen. I let three years go by; was it all worth it? Not talking to her because she had a problem that I could not fix? I don't know how I should feel. Should I be joyful or deeply saddened by not caring? I love my sister, and I lost her because my mother could not kick a bad habit.

Do I pray to God to give me another miracle? Maybe this time it won't be for abundance. I would exchange that dream for a clean bill of health. I have twenty-eight days, and I guess all that is left is to live life with no limits and no more regrets.

Marisa

Congratulations

Marisa invites Melinda and Sarah over to eat pizza and watch a movie. She, along with her roommate, Janice, tells them the news. The girls talk and chat until Marisa starts to tell them what has been going on since the time they all bought their lottery tickets.

"I have some news to tell all of you."

Melinda asks whether it is good news or bad news. Marisa, wishing that she could change the subject, knows she has to be transparent and tell them the truth, although she hates having emotions in general.

"The good news is that I won the lottery."

15

Melinda and Sarah start hugging and jumping around in a big circle to the point where Marisa cannot say anything in between their excitement, so to calm the mood, she yells the bad news of her having cancer.

Melinda and Sarah both stop. They and Janice all look worried and quickly give their attention to Marisa again.

"I called you all over here for that reason. I don't want you to feel sorry for me. This made me think what would be the best way to spend my last days with my friends, and I figured it would be seeing the world."

The girls are still quiet and are not sure what to say or how to respond to anything coming out of Marisa's mouth.

Marisa says, "Seriously, think of it like this: any dream we have ever had, if money can buy it, then we're doing it. Name a city outside the country that we all want to go to."

The girls take a few minutes to think. They put a bunch of city and country names in a hat. The hat is filled with countries and cities, and each of the girls pulls a name out of the hat to find the four places that they will visit.

Sarah pulls out Paris, Melinda pulls out Italy, and Janice dips her hand in and takes Amsterdam. Marisa, nervous pulling hers out as this might be the last thing her eyes see, pulls out Tokyo.

Marisa says, "Let's go. We'll buy clothes at each destination. First stop is Paris. There's a limo outside waiting for us."

Janice and Melinda both look outside to see if Marisa is telling the truth. They see an all-black limo outside with the driver by the door, waiting for the girls' arrival downstairs. Marisa smiles after her witty statement and leaves the apartment. The rest of the girls look at one another and then look out the window to see Marisa walk into the limousine. Then her friends follow.

Paris

Paris has amazing historical places to check out: the Eiffel Tower and Montmartre, as well as Notre Dame. Paris tourism is big; millions of people come every year. Paris is considered by many to be the center of art.

All the girls are excited riding first-class, feeling comfortable, and they ask for champagne from the flight attendant. While the flight attendants are giving instructions, the girls fall asleep.

They wake up when the plane arrives at Charles de Gaulle Airport.

As the girls are checking into the Mandarin Hotel, Marisa has a conversation with the concierge to book a room for her and the girls.

"Can I help you, madam?"

"Yes, you can. I'd like to book a room."

"All our regular rooms are booked. I'm sorry."

"That's fine. I actually want the best room you have available."

"That will be a thousand dollars a night."

"That's fine," Marisa says and hands him her debit card. The concierge is shocked that someone her age did not try to ask for a manager or someone to dispute the price of that room.

The concierge's eyes become as large as the black holes that exist in space. He then cracks his knuckles and rolls his neck before he starts to take down her information for the room.

After a few minutes of admiring the lobby of the hotel, the girls go up the elevator to their room, where they are amazed at the view and cannot wait to create memories in Paris.

All the girls are moving around, checking out the penthouse, opening up the minibar, until Marisa takes control of the situation.

"Don't touch the minibar! I'm rich and I'm going to die, but I'm not stupid. OK, so we're in Paris. What are we going to do?"

Sarah says, "We can go see the Eiffel Tower."

Melinda says, "Why would we do that if we already accomplished that by being right next door to the Eiffel Tower? Look!"

Marisa has a funny smirk before she comments on what they can do in Paris. The look that is in her face is the wicked smile that you can usually find on a bully waiting for a wimpy kid to take advantage of.

Marisa says, "A lot of people go to the Eiffel Tower. Not many people throw eggs at those heading to the Eiffel Tower."

When that was said, the girls had a devilish smirk across their faces as if they were kids that were up to no good.

Operation Eiffel

Marisa and all the girls have walkie-talkies and are at different posts all around the Eiffel Tower. Marisa and Janice are up on the top of their hotel building, and Melinda and Sarah are on the bottom with the people by the Eiffel Tower.

Marisa says, "OK, girls, Operation Eiffel is officially on in five, four, three, two, one, go."

Sarah says to Marisa and Lisa, "OK, I see our first target, the man with the trench coat. As soon as you throw that egg, you both need to go quarter clockwise before the guards see who threw the eggs."

Marisa throws the egg and watches the egg hit the man's trench coach. The man is confused at what is going on. Both girls hide, and when he looks away again, Janice throws her egg. Both the eggs have now hit the man in the trench coat. Sarah tells them to move counterclockwise to stay away from the guard and look for a new target.

Melinda says, "OK, I got this one, you guys. See that man wearing that ugly shirt? I think he needs more than that brown color. Hit him as soon as you guys have a shot."

The man is wearing a brown shirt that could pass for a bowel movement in the girls' eyes and needs something to brighten up the shirt: a bit of yellow.

Janice and Marisa do their eggs together this time. They do a countdown, and as soon as they say "one," they both let go of their eggs. Sarah confirms that it is a hit.

The third target, wearing a red-and-white striped shirt, is hit in his face. All the girls laugh, and their cover is blown as numerous people start pointing up at them as they are figured out by the growing crowd.

Sarah and Melinda leave their post and start walking really fast to the hotel, leaving Marisa and Janice to meet them back at the room. As soon as Marisa and Janice hear the call from the walkie-talkie, they dash for the stairs. The security guard cannot stop them as he is a second late, the door closing in his face.

They get off the rooftop, sprint back to their room, and knock on the door, where Sarah and Melinda cannot stop laughing about how much fun that prank was.

Day Two of Paris

The girls are up early in the lobby, sitting on the couch, thinking of what they can do for their second day in Paris. Janice has the bright idea that if they have a few shots at the hotel bar, it can help spark their brains to see what they can do to have fun for their second day in Paris.

The girls have a sudden urge to drink after they realize they don't have to wake up to do anything of importance but live. So they decide to experience losing control and start drinking tequila while everyone else is in a coffee shop drinking a small shot of espresso in the morning they are at the Hotel bar.

Sarah says, "Oh God, I can only imagine how we're going to feel after this."

Marisa says, "We're going to feel great. Let's start off at the hotel lounge, shall we?"

The girls are the only ones at the hotel bar so early, and they all take shots of tequila.

Sarah starts making a funny noise while saying the words "I think I'm drunk." Marisa and Janice moved gingerly as they try to keep up with Melinda. The girls' bright idea suddenly misfires; they think they are going to different bars, only to find out they have been in the same bar the whole time, too drunk to be seen in public. The girls agree this was a bad idea and a process of sobering up is needed before they see a bit more of Paris and head for Italy.

After a few hours of drinking water and eating bread to sober up, the girls decide to go shopping and see a fashion show being held. They received tickets to the show by being guests at the hotel.

The girls are fashionably late, sitting down and watching a few of the models pass. As the models pass while everyone is having a good time, Marisa has a flashback to the last class with Professor Morry.

Professor Morry had said, "I want to know what you would want to do with your last month. As humans, we are naive to think we will always have time, when the truth is that every day, time is ticking."

Marisa is being called by Sarah to snap out of it as the fashion show is over. She now snaps out of her flashback and starts to walk out of the show with the other girls.

24 Days Left

Four days have passed, and I have loved every moment. I love feeling free, not being constricted, not feeling obligated. Paris was great. I hope Italy enhances the feeling of living the way Paris just did for me. I got to re-experience many feelings and ages in just four days. The years I thought were stripped from me felt like they all just came back. On this flight my mind has been wandering on what can happen in our few days in Italy. We're going to be in Venice. I know it should be a great time; I can't wait for me and my girls to create new memories. There's something about the thought of Italy that makes me want to know about its culture, the essence of family. I know these are all stereotypes, but for some reason, on this journey, I hope most of it is true.

Marisa

Italy

Italy has a population of over sixty million people. A fun fact about this country is that Italy is slightly larger than the state of Arizona. It is hemmed in by four nations: France, Switzerland, and Austria, as well as Slovenia.

Marisa and the girls get on a charter jet to head to Italy.

Marisa says, "How you ladies like the jet?"

Melinda says, "Don't you think this is a little much, Marisa?"

"Relax; I haven't even spent a million dollars yet. We're just getting started."

Marisa has a big smile on her face as the plane takes off for Italy. The stewardess comes around to offer the ladies a drink.

The girls finally make it to their destination and are now checking into their hotel in Italy.

Marisa has just finished checking into the hotel when an older woman gets an attitude when she finds out the girls booked her standard suite. She gives the concierge a hard time.

The concierge says, "I'm sorry your room has been booked, Ms. Hart."

"What do you mean, it's been booked? That's the only room I use when I'm in town."

"Yes, that is the room. Someone booked the room before you. They asked for this suite prior to your request."

"I'm not allowed to give this information. I hope you do understand, Ms. Hart."

"No, I don't. I want to see a manager. Do you know who I am?"

The concierge nervously, in a timid voice, says he does in fact know who she is and will be more than happy to get a manager.

Ms. Hart says, "Good, a manager!" She is making a big scene complaining, and while doing that, she is ringing the bell at the front desk. Marisa looks at her in disgust and walks away. Marisa has now found someone whose life she and her girls can make miserable during their stay in Italy. She wants to make sure she will never be forgotten by Ms. Hart for giving the concierge such a hard time when he was only trying to do his job.

This gives them a motive for their new prank.

The girls are getting acclimated in their new room, where they are talking amongst themselves.

Janice asks, "What are we going to do in Italy?"

Sarah says, "Easy. Check out the sights in Venice."

Melinda says, "No, we need to handle that lady that was so mean to the concierge. She was a little ridiculous. Don't you think?"

Marisa says, "You just read my mind. I think we need to order room service."

"What are you talking about? We just ate."

"Not for us but for Ms. Hart. First things first, we're going to go downstairs and give the concierge the idea we have in mind with a little incentive."

Sarah agrees to the idea and figures she will designate herself to talk to the concierge.

As Sarah is going down, she sees the concierge that was being scolded by Ms. Hart; his manager eventually showed up to do the same. Sarah watches him and thinks about how to go into the situation; he seems a little upset that he got scolded by his manager, even though what he did was proper protocol. Sarah then walks up to him with a pleasant smile before she speaks to him.

"Hey, how are you? I'm sorry about that lady. She had no right treating you like that for doing your job."

"Yeah, but I knew I should have booked you guys in a different suite."

"Hey, you were doing the right thing, and that's why my friends and I want to help pay you back for giving us the best room in the hotel."

Intrigued by the proposition, he asks how, with an eagerness to find out. Sarah whispers that she needs a bellhop's outfit, as well as Ms. Hart's room number and a phone call as soon as Ms. Hart orders room service. He agrees he can do just that.

Sarah says thanks and goes back to the suite to devise the plan.

Marisa says, "OK, the plan is simple now that Sarah did her part. When we find out Ms. Hart ordered food, we will put worms on a plate so she will scream and freak out. From there, Melinda is going to do 'dingdong ditch' to have

Ms. Hart step out of the room. We're going to put two ice buckets full of flour on her when she opens the door. That will give us all enough time to ditch the area."

The girls agree with the plan, and now it's in motion. Sarah gets the call, and Operation Miserable Hart is in full effect.

Melinda knocks on the door, changes out of the concierge outfit, and hands it to Janice. Ms. Hart is in her room and has just finished ordering room service. Sarah is now walking through the hallway, trying to stay low-key and keep her face from being seen by too many cameras. Melinda approaches the door, knocks, and screams "Room service!" in her best male voice. She runs off in the opposite direction of the way the girls are looking to hear the prank unfold.

Ms. Hart says, "I just ordered this food. It cannot be ready." She shrugs her shoulders and brings in the tray, and as soon as she opens up the tray, she jumps up and screams in shock as there are now worms moving on the table. She gets so scared that her hand swipes at the table, knocking the tray to the floor. She jumps on the bed and starts screaming very loud. The girls start laughing as they hear the screams all the way down the hall. As Ms. Hart runs out of the room, the girls throw a bucket of flour in her face.

They all flee the scene and laugh all the way to their room.

Marisa and the girls are now checking out the famous Trevi Fountain, taking photos and just enjoying the sights, when Marisa sees the man of her dreams.

Luke is in his early twenties and has a charming smile. He notices that Marisa's friends are egging her on to go over and speak with him. Luke notices this, walks over to Marisa, and introduces himself. While Luke tries to talk to Marisa Sarah interrupts by answering questions that were intended for Marisa.

Luke says, "Hi, how you all doing?"

Sarah says, "We're fine. How are you?"

"Good. Where are you all from? I can hear your accents."

"Yeah, we're from the States."

"Not to be rude, but I was talking to your friend." Luke greets Marisa with a handshake. "I'm Luke."

"Marisa Nice to meet you, Luke"

"I don't mean to seem too forward, but how long are you going to be in Italy?"

"Not too long. We're just here for a few days."

"I guess that means I should take you to dinner."

Marisa nervously says, "That sounds nice and all, but I don't think I can do that, you see."

Sarah says, "Yes, you can. Pick her up at eight thirty." Sarah gets a pen and writes down the address on Luke's hand. "You can pick her up from this address. Don't be late."

"I won't. See you tonight." Luke now walks away with a smile.

Luke and Marisa

Luke knocks on the door of the girls' hotel suite, and Sarah opens the door. She lets Luke in and waits to see Marisa get out the bathroom to see how Marisa looks for the date.

Melinda says, "Marisa! Hurry up. You have company."

Janice is putting the finishing touches on Marisa's hair. She says, "You gonna look good."

"It's whatever. I'm just being nice to him."

"Yeah, OK, you know you want to go. You tired of us. Hell, I'm tired of myself. Too much estrogen."

Marisa and Janice start laughing, but Marisa does not want to keep Luke waiting. She is concerned about what might be next to come out of Jessica's mouth. Marisa rushes over, interrupts Jessica's next sentence, and grabs Luke by the arm; together they are now heading out of the hotel to enjoy the evening.

Marisa and Luke are at Antica Pesca. The waiter finishes taking their order and walks away. Luke tries to break the ice, to find common ground, by asking about family, but before Luke can get to that subject, Marisa cuts him off. She is insecure about why someone as handsome as Luke would take the time to want to be with her.

Marisa says, "I have a question."

"Yes, anything."

"Why me?"

"Why you what?"

"You know this fancy restaurant. I'm sure you took other girls here." Marisa is timid and cautious. She does not want to get hurt or appear to seem weak or like a girl that can be taken advantage of for being a tourist.

Luke says, "No, I haven't. The reason why I wanted to go out to eat with you is because of your smile. Although I know we never met before, I just feel like you're a good person. Something just told me that I had to speak to you, as if I could make Italy a bit more special than just sight-seeing."

After Luke compliment Marisa on her beauty, she cannot help but smile and feel flattered. The food has come out from the kitchen. They both start to eat and continue to have a conversation about various topics such as pet peeves and favorite things to do.

After dinner the two continue their conversation, walking toward the hotel until they see a gelateria where they can both find a reason to keep this date going a little longer. Marisa is glad to have contact with the opposite sex and not just her friends.

Luke asks, "What's your favorite gelato?"

"Pistachio."

"Then why did you buy chocolate?"

"Because it is the next best thing to what I prefer."

Luke laughs at Marisa's whit; he finds it very enchanting. "I like to keep it simple."

"Simple—that feels like something you do not do."

"What, simple?"

"Yeah, you just met me this afternoon, and you already wined and dined me at a restaurant where I can't pronounce anything on the menu. That's not simple."

"Maybe I think you're worth complicating things for," Luke says with a smile.

Marisa, with little to no confidence, mumbles under her breath, "I doubt that."

"Why do you think you're not worth feeling complicated for?"

"Let's just say it's complicated."

"OK, but complicated can be good if it's me and you."

Marisa says in a frantic voice, "Not like this, Luke. Trust me. Thank you for dinner. It was the best date I have ever had. Good night."

Luke, trying to change her tone of voice, asks if they can do brunch. Marisa smiles and goes for a kiss on the cheek, when Luke moves his cheek so both their lips are in sync. Marisa continues to kiss him longer than what he is expecting.

"'Night, Luke."

Marisa walks through the doors into the hotel lobby, where the girls are waiting for her to ask her how the date went.

Janice, "Hold on, let me get the popcorn. I need to hear this story." Marisa sits on the couch and starts to mention everything that happened on the date. She talks about how much of a gentleman Luke is and how she wishes she could spend more time in Italy, but she wants to see more of the world.

22 Days Left

I have only a day left in Italy, and I love the scenery here. It is so peaceful and relaxing. I love the journey I am on. I just wish things wouldn't have to end.

I wish it were all meaningful, that I could know what love is, what love would feel like if I had more time. Everything right now is a fairy tale with an unenviable ending. I am going to die in twenty-two days.

There is no way to sugarcoat the changes in my life. It is what it is: I am going to die. I hate the feeling of wanting to open up, but what's the point? There is nothing to open up for.

I have nothing but money; that means nothing. The things I valued never came true. I want to reconnect with my mother. I want to find my sister, but there is no need to feel loved when

I am going to leave them. Am I being selfish? Or am I protecting myself? I hope death is just sleeping and not waking up.

Did I live, or was I just alive? Did I get a chance to serve the world the way I was supposed to? Did I give enough, or did I just take?

Marisa

Last Day in Italy

Marisa and Luke are spending time together in the city of Milan. Marisa is amazed by all the history and things there are to see. The city has a population a bit more than a million. It was founded by the Insubres, who were eventually conquered by the Romans. Marisa is amazed at how beautiful this place can still look even after being at the forefront of World War II. Marisa feels blessed to have Luke take the time to help immerse her in his culture and this city on the south coast of Italy.

Luke takes her to historical structures like the Royal Villa and the Terrazze del Duomo, where they walked on the terrace taking in the breath taking views over Milan where you can admire one of the most beautiful cathedrals in Italy. The cathedral is touching for Marisa; how beautiful and grand it looks. She closes her eyes and says a prayer she was taught as a little girl by her mother, before her mother changed. It is the Prayer of Jabez.

"Oh, that you would bless me indeed, and enlarge my territory, that your hand would be with me and that you would keep me from evil, that I may not cause pain."

They also have an artist draw them a portrait, which awkwardly makes her miss home; she is used to street artists doing portraits on Forty-Second Street, with a bunch of costume-wearing adults taking photos as the neighborhood Spider-Man, as well as Mickey and Minnie Mouse, and a Tickle Me Elmo always in sight.

After a spiritual and inspiring day, Luke and Marisa return to the hotel in the evening to see the stars in Venice.

Marisa is in such a joyful place. She thanks Luke for such an amazing day. "Thank you so much."

Luke, trying to be modest, does not say much but holds her body tightly and says, "Thank you for what?"

Marisa says, "This. You made the last few days amazing."

"Well, you are amazing, and that's just it. When can I come to America to see you?"

"Luke, this is more than likely the last time you're going to see me."

Marisa starts to get disheartened. She does not want to talk about her situation and knows that if she does, she will be completely shattered. Marisa knows her answers won't be sufficient without delving deeper knowing it will only make sense to Luke if she opens up to talk about her life

What Marisa loves about this situation is not receiving pity. Luke likes her for being her, not for being sick and soon to die. She wants to hold on to that feeling of someone not

46

knowing what the next few weeks will be like for her.

Marisa says, "I don't really feel like talking about it."

Luke, getting more confused by the second, asks, "Why not? It can't be that bad."

"It can be. Let's just enjoy the moment."

"You don't get it, Marisa. I want this moment forever."

"I wish I could tell you something more reassuring, but I can't. This is all nice, but I knew this would happen. I have to go."

Marisa then gives Luke a kiss and leaves Luke there by himself. She has the same feelings as Luke does but is too afraid to show them because there will be nothing after tonight.

21 Days Left

I feel so many emotions today. I feel joy, love, sadness, angriness, loneliness, and irritation. He brings out emotions in me I thought only my mother could bring out in me.

I feel joy because of Luke. He is so charming and nice and has an amazing outlook on life. He is someone I wish I could spend the last days of my life with. This brings me to the feeling of love. I liked guys before but not like this. It is much deeper. I feel vulnerable as I cannot protect myself around him. I feel weak in his presence. Not weak from not feeling independent, but more from admiring his qualities I would want my son to learn from him if I could have children.

I feel sad that my one shot at a romantic love story was stripped away from me. I'm sad that I am going to die. I am sad that I have a mother who I don't get along with. I'm sad that my sister may never know how much I love her.

I feel anger towards God as I feel I have no control over my life. What did I do to deserve this? Did I receive a curse from doing something in my past, or am I paying for the pain of others' sin?

Did someone pray for me to have my happiest day becoming my saddest day all at the same time?

I feel lonely. I can share my money with anyone, but who can I share my thoughts with? The feeling of being lonely and having my best friends around me has me at a very low place in my life. I go there a lot in my mind; more often now knowing my days are numbered. It makes me question what life is. Is it this place to show us pain so we can appreciate heaven, or is it just a feeling of wanting something missing, like a spiritual being? Or maybe the loneliness is because of the feeling of me needing and wanting God to get me through. It felt great going to the cathedral. It's one of the few times I took the time to have solitude, with my innermost thoughts although Luke was there.

Irritated that I cannot change the course of my life, but knowing my friends will keep my memory alive keeps me going. Writing this at the airport, although it saddens me. I know I need to feel everything life has to offer. I do not want any stones unturned.

Marisa

Amsterdam

Amsterdam is the capital of the Netherlands. The population of Amsterdam is less than a million people. Amsterdam has one of the most famous red light districts. Its nickname is "Mokum," which is Hebrew for "place" or "city."

The girls are in Amsterdam, ready to have the time of their lives. They look around the local market, and Janice has the bright idea to buy brownies from a shop saying "organic recipes." The word "organic" is another way of promoting "special" brownies.

Lisa, completely unaware of this, believes this is a great idea. The girls are not so quick to join Lisa, although they too are hungry.

Janice asks, "Can we please stop and get something to eat? I'm hungry."

Sarah says, "What are you trying to eat?"

"Something small. You know, like a snack. A friend told me if you ever come to Amsterdam, find a market that sells organic brownies. They're really healthy for you."

As Janice says that, she walks into the market. Melinda, Marisa, and Sarah follow.

The clerk is a nice, older woman who has a bright smile and moves very gingerly. This reminds Marisa of when she was a child, seeing her mom in pain due to an injury at work. The girls, after a few minutes of small talk with the elderly clerk, buy the brownies. It takes only an hour before the brownies get to them. Instead of being in a laid-back mood, the girls decide to drink and throw a party among themselves.

All the girls react differently to the brownies. The girls have a small party, doing crazy and bizarre things. There is a stray dog that sneaks into their room. They drink homemade jungle juice. Jungle juice consists of pineapple and mango juice, Sprite, Hawaiian Punch, vodka, peach schnapps, rum, triple sec, gin, strawberry wine, and lastly, sour apple pucker that was mixed by the girls. Janice is listening to reggae music on the couch. Marisa keeps trying to see her reflection in the jungle juice bowl that was made

Sarah is in her own world with her hands in her pants, trying to act manly, walking around the room. Melinda is looking and begging someone to order food as she has the munchies mixed with high intoxication.

She says, "I'm so hungry. Let's order something." She picks up the phone to order room service and listens to what everyone is shouting to place their order.

Before the food can arrive, all the girls are sleeping. Room service knocks on the door many times, trying to get an answer.

Sisterhood

All the girls head to the lobby, where they all sit on a couch to discuss their favorite parts of the trip so far. All talk about the bond that this trip has brought them.

Marisa says, "I really want to thank you guys."

Sarah and Janice ask what they are being thanked for.

Marisa, without trying to seem so sentimental, wants to show gratitude for their spending the last few weeks with her before she dies.

Sarah responds, "We should be thanking you."

Janice agrees. "Yeah, without you winning the lottery, we would not be able to see the finer things in life."

Marisa thinks out loud to her friends. "Is this really the finer things in life? Cramming your dreams all in one month?"

She continues, "Where is my journey? Where is my legacy? Money can buy a lot of dreams, but some dreams come with time. Unfortunately, time is something I don't have."

All the girls are speechless as they listen to each word Marisa has to say. Marisa notices and wants to ease the tension and change the vibe of the room by finishing her thoughts. "What I am trying to say is that you are my sisters, and I would not want to share this journey with anyone else but you guys."

Marisa then asks, "What's everyone's favorite part of the trip?"

Melinda says, "I enjoyed Paris. The prank we played was hilarious."

Sarah says, "I enjoyed the sights of Italy. And when I say the sights, I mean the men."

The girls start to laugh at Sarah.

Janice says, "Not to sound mushy, because I can't stand it when you guys do it, but the memories of Marisa. I got to see her feel free and liberated. Who would have thought me and my best friend since five would see the world together?"

Marisa says, "Like I said before, thanks, you guys, for making my last days on this earth a memorable one."

Sarah says, "Enough of you girls being Debbie Downers. Let's get out of here."

The girls get up. Marisa leaves money on the table to cover the tab, and they go back upstairs to relax and kick up their feet.

19 Days Left

According to my doctor, I have nineteen days: two week and five days. I'm starting to become numb to the feeling of death. I hope there is a heaven, and I hope I appreciate Heaven when the time comes. I took life for granted. I love the bond that I have with Melinda, Sarah, and Janice. They treat me like nothing is wrong, and I am so grateful for that. I am still on the fence about reaching out to my mother. I want to tell her that I am going to die, that she will never see me again, that I am no longer a girl: I died a woman. I want my sister to know that I love her and I'm deeply sorry I could not keep her away from what her eyes saw. Eleven days, and all that will be left behind is money. I can never spend all of it. This book with my thoughts—when I die, I want my friends to read this book so they can know where I was mentally on this journey. I want those that loved me to remember me as someone that was unselfish, charismatic, and always up for a good time. I hope this is all felt when they speak at my funeral.

Marisa

Prank in Amsterdam

The girls are on the balcony drinking a cool beverage, plotting what should be the prank of Amsterdam. The girls have pulled a prank in all of the places they have been to so far—Paris and Italy—and Amsterdam will be no different.

Marisa says, "Everywhere we went, we pulled a prank. What's our prank for Amsterdam?"

Sarah says, "We should make our own version of special brownies."

Melinda asks, "What do you mean, 'our own special brownies'?"

Janice says, "Yeah, that's going to give them the time of their lives. Not anything that we can laugh about, just relaxing."

Sarah asks, "Who said the brownies were going to have weed in them?"

The girls all smile after hearing Sarah make the suggestion of creating a laxative brownie. The prank seems like a great idea to the girls, and Sarah is in the forefront to make sure that this prank is pulled off.

The girls decide that their target will be the employees of the hotel. The brownies are taken out the oven by Jessica. The recipe for these brownies consists of self-rising flour, powdered sugar, two eggs, three tablespoons of chocolate powder, and butter—and of course, laxatives mixed into the tasteful mix. After the brownies are baked, the girls walk to all the employees in the hotel lobby, offering the brownies,

Sarah says, "Hi, we bought you and the staff some brownies just to say thank you for making this a home away from home."

The concierge says, "No problem, any time. If there is anything we can do, please let I or anyone from the staff know, we will do our best to accommodate you girls."

The concierge, an older gentleman, takes a bite. He's so delighted by the taste he eats another.

Some staff members even ask for two because they are so delicious.

Thirty minutes later, all the employees start trying to fight one another to make it to the bathroom while the girls just watch everything happening and find this to be their entertainment.

Melinda says, "Damn, we got them good. Maybe a little too good."

Sarah says, "Yeah, we did, but it was well worth it."

Marisa says, "I actually feel really bad we did something like that."

Melinda says, "I don't know why. Everywhere we go, these hotel agencies always give us a hard time for a hotel room, always throwing the prices in our face."

Marisa says, "Don't let that get to you. We get them back every time."

Sarah says, "We sure do."

The girls walk out of the lobby after watching their prank play out.

Janice asks, "So what's next?"

Marisa says, "Whatever we want to do."

Melinda says, "Let's go De Negen Straatjes (The Nine Little Streets) We need to hit the town and go party one good time in Amsterdam."

Remembering the Moment

After shopping during the midday, the girls are now ready to live the nightlife in Amsterdam. The girls are excited to spend their last night in Amsterdam in a club they heard good things about from the locals. Marisa pays for VIP treatment; there is a waitress on call, and five bottles are on ice for them.

Janice says, "Can't believe it's our last night in Amsterdam already."

Melinda says, "Yeah, me too. Let's just enjoy our last night here."

After drinking a multitude of drinks and just dancing, having a fun time, Marisa has a moment in her own world having a flash back, remembering the first day of her new life when Dr. Lehman told her the worst news on a day that should have been the greatest as a lottery winner. Dr. Lehman had walked in, taken a deep breath, and looked at Marisa in the eye to the point where Marisa got nervous.

Marisa said, "Dr. Lehman, what's wrong?"

Dr. Lehman said, "Marisa, there is no easy way to say this, so I am going to just come right out and say it."

Marisa, scared of what was to be said, braced herself and said, "OK."

Dr. Lehman said, "With the CAT scan, we found a tumor that we cannot get to. In our estimation, you have three weeks—if you're lucky, a month—to live."

Melinda taps Marisa's shoulder to get her attention. Marisa finally snaps out of it and realizes that people are leaving and people are cleaning up the club. The girls leave the club to head back to the hotel room to pack their bags and head to their last destination: Japan.

Japan

Japan has a population around 127 million. Japan is an island in East Asia. Most people in Japan are avid lovers of baseball.

The girls start their adventure in Tokyo as they are in a cab driving, enjoying the nighttime sky. Looking at the city lights reminds them of Times Square.

Melinda says, "This is a smaller New York."

Sarah says, "Even though we visited all these amazing places, none of them are New York, you know."

Janice says, "The last few weeks have been a, dream come true, if you think about it. Marisa manifested it. She said she was going to win the lottery and she did."

Marisa says, "What do you mean, Janice"

"Remember when we were twelve and we used to go to the rooftop?"

"Yeah, why?"

"Remember what you said?"

"'The day I visit different parts of the world, I can die.' I guess I cursed myself."

"No, Marisa, you made the impossible possible. How many people get the opportunity to say their last memories were all filled with best friends?"

Marisa smiles at the wisdom of her best friend giving her enlightenment on the experience. Marisa knows that as much as this is a blessing, she wishes she could refund the money for time. Marisa now understands that money cannot buy happiness.

17 Days Left

I haven't told any of the girls, but I'm starting to feel very ill. I've been losing feeling in my hand. I can barely pick up this pen to write. My migraines have been more apparent than what I've been accustomed to. I hope the girls won't be upset, but I think we need to cut the trip a few days short. I need to make it back home. I need to speak to my mom. I need to bury the hatchet on any problems I have with my mom. I need to find a way to see my sister before my time. I need to write a letter to my dad. I need to clear my conscience, and I cannot do that in Japan. I have to go home to make this all happen.

Marisa

Marisa complains to the girls about her migraine. She starts dozing in and out in their Tokyo hotel room. She eventually faints, and the girls crowd around her, scrambling to her side to get an ambulance.

Janice says, "Oh my God, Marisa, wake up." Janice slaps her face to try and wake her up. The girls huddle in a panic, wanting to wake her up. While being knocked unconscious, Marisa instantly dreams of the last conversation she had with her father before he left the family.

"Dad, where you going?"

"To the store."

"Dad?"

"Yes?"

"Can you get me some candy please?"

"Yes, sweetie."

The younger Marisa has such an angelic smile and can easily tell she idolized her father with knowing she was Daddy's girl.

Marisa wakes up in a hospital in Japan. She is in the bed, her friends waiting for her to wake up. When she does, the girls are relieved, and a doctor comes in to speak about the reasoning behind this.

Doctor Kiro speaks very little English and lacks sympathy.

"I'm Kiro," he says. "How are you feeling?"

Marisa responds"A little woozy."

"Are you familiar with your tumor?"

"Yes."

"So you know you die?"

"Yes. Do you know how much time?"

"Around three days."

Marisa starts to cry, and the girls do their best to console Marisa about the news from Dr. Kiro.

Janice says, "Hey, Marisa, what do you want to do?"

Melinda says, "Don't let that doctor get you down."

Marisa says, "I know, I know. It's just really scary to know that it's all coming to an end."

All the girls get emotional and feel the pain in Marisa's voice as she talks about her dream way to die.

"I see myself watching one of my childhood movies on repeat. I envision my mother checking in on me, my sister sitting next to me, my dad making popcorn on top of the stove.

We used to all watch Snow White and the Seven Dwarfs. I could watch that movie all day because that's the last memory I had of when my family was whole.

Home Sweet Home

Marisa and the girls are back in New York. She is on the rooftop thinking. Janice comes up to check on her.

Janice says, "Hey, girl. You OK?"

"Yeah, I'm OK."

"What you doing here?"

"Just thinking."

"About?"

"My last days."

"Oh, I'm sorry. I'll leave you alone."

"No, it's OK. I'm glad you are here."

Janice, not knowing what to say, puts her hand on Marisa's shoulder to show compassion but feels awkward not knowing how or having the right words to help out her best friend.

Marisa says, "You know, I was thinking: What's so great about life if I have no one to tell my story?"

"What do you mean? You have me, Sarah, and Melinda to tell your story."

"Yeah, but there are so many things I was not able to do."

"You won the lottery. We saw the world in three weeks. What else were you not able to do?"

Marisa, frustrated that Janice does not understand her frustration, gets angry to the point where her eyes start to shed tears, before screaming, "I was not able to fall in love! I wasn't able to have children! I wasn't able to reconnect with my father! Money can buy a lot of things, but some moments only come with time. That's what I want: time." Marisa then walking off the rooftop gingerly, as her motor movements are slowing down.

My Last Day

Today feels like my last day on this earth. I hope I did what God had planned for me. I hope these letters will keep me in the memory of all my loved ones. I hope everyone and anyone that reads this gets inspired to live life better than I did. I hope my best friends read this, and I hope my mother knows I forgive her, and I hope my sister can forgive me.

Mom, I love you, and I know you did your best to raise me and Ally. I know you meant well even through your addiction to your prescription medication limited you. I haven't been the best daughter. I blamed you for Dad leaving us. I have the same level of patience, which is not saying much.

Ally, I love you so much. I'm sorry I couldn't raise you and the state came and intervened.

Please understand that Mom really needed help, and I got emancipated, and that was selfish of me. I wish I could tell you in person but do not have the strength to do so. Even with this potentially being my last words to everyone I care for, I still can't build up enough courage to tell you or anyone my feelings.

To Sarah, Melinda, and Janice, besides my sister, you three are my sisters. You guys treated me the same after I told you about my illness. If my journal is confusing to you, it's because it is also confusing to me. Right now I am going to break down everything you guys just read, from the trips we never went on, to where you can find the ticket.

I did win the lottery. When you turn to the last page of the book, you will see the key to the PO box number and which post office to go to: retrieve the winning ticket with the rules that come along with it.

The Girls rush to the Post office to open up the PO Box and read the rest of Marisa's wishes.

I went on this journey in my mind these last weeks, this journey of what would be the best way to leave this earth, and although I will never be able to do it physically, I hope you will visit the places I talked about. I want you all to pull a prank in every city, and I want you girls to find my sister and have her take my place on this trip. I want her to know what life is like with women like you.

If there's one thing I want you all to remember, it is that time should not be taken for granted. I have written what I wish I had done for my last days of my life with the sisters I love. I felt it was more important to write this notebook of what I wanted you to do in my memory. My dad always said I was lucky. I guess my winning proves that point. I'm sure there was a better chance of having cancer than of winning the lottery; I did both. Cancer was a blessing; it showed me that everything I needed was in front of me. I had loyal friends that stayed by my side. I found people that truly loved me. I wish I had met a man before I left this earth, but we can't have it all, and that's what I learned. Appreciate your journey and make an impact on your journey. I'm going through all this pain, which will make me appreciate heaven, so for that, God knew exactly what he was doing, and for that, I am so grateful.

I love you all, and please never forget about me on your journey. Keep me in your heart while God now has my spirit. I love you all.

Marisa

Farewell, Marisa

The girls are all in the post office, where they are reading the notebook that has some of Marisa's most intimate thoughts. The girls are in chills after reading the book that Marisa has written as if she were a third person, as well as in a journal format. With the girls now having this information, they make a plan to meet with Marisa's mom and to find Marisa's sister. The girls never knew she had a younger sister, except Janice, who was sworn to secrecy by Marisa that she would never mention anything about Ally.

The girls figure the plan will be to find Ally. Finding Marisa's sister first, they will let her read the book and let her know about the lottery ticket, and although she is underage, they will make sure Ally will have a trust fund set up. The girls agree that Janice will sign Ally's last name on the ticket, and Janice will see if she can become Ally's legal guardian until Ally is eighteen. Janice knows where Marisa's mother lives and so decides to go visit her to let her know that Marisa passed yesterday and see if she has any information that can help the girls find out more about Ally.

Marisa's mom, Janet, lives on 118th Street between Fourth and Fifth Avenues. Janice walks up the stairs, and in doing so, she sees hustlers in the building and a pregnant woman who just gave money to receive drugs. Janice makes sure she keeps her eye contact to a minimum until she reaches the second floor, where she then knocks on the apartment 4H.

Janice knocks on the door twice to make sure her knock can be heard. Janet says, "Hold on." As Janice waits, she looks around and takes a deep breath to be prepared to tell Janet about Marisa.

Janet says, "Oh my God, Janice, is that you?"

"Yes, it is. How you are?"

"God answered my prayer. I was hoping to run into you so I could ask you about Marisa."

"That's exactly why I came here. Do you mind if I come in, Ms. Janet?"

"Sure, absolutely. Please forgive me for the mess. You caught me in the midst of straightening up the living room."

Janet is wobbling as she had a bad accident at work that caused her addiction to pain-killers and the rift between her and Marisa.

Janet says, "So what brings you by, Lisa?"

"Well, there are a few things. One, I need you to brace yourself. It's about Marisa."

"OK, what is it?"

"Marisa passed away yesterday and had a book with wishes to be completed. She did not tell you about her condition. However, she wanted it to be known that she loves you and forgives you. She said she was selfish even to the point of not having the courage to tell you that she was dying."

Janice feels relieved after getting that off her chest. Janet is stone cold with slight tears coming out of her eyes. She is processing all that was just said.

The room is so quiet that you can hear the next-door neighbor's children watching cartoons. Janet grabs a piece of tissue from her coffee table to wipe her eyes.

Janet says, "Is she having a funeral?"

"She requested that she be cremated and that a few of us spread her remains in a few locations that she asked for me and her friends to keep between us."

"I know I wasn't the best mother, but I tried."

"And Marisa noticed that and wanted to make sure that you knew that she loved you and knew that you did your absolute best, especially when your husband left."

"OK, what else did you want to find out?"

"I wanted to know if you have a way to contact Ally."

Janet does not say a word. She walks across the room to a bookshelf, where she has the information that Janice asked for. She wobbles like a penguin back to her seat, where she takes a deep breath and opens to the bookmarked page that says where Ally is.

Janet says, "She is at the Washington Heights Group Home. You talk to someone there, and you can more than likely tell her about Marisa and whatever else may need to be said. Visiting hours are three to seven Monday through Friday."

"Thank you, Ms. Janet, for this information, and I'm really sorry."

"Don't be sorry. I should have done my part to try to find my daughter when I got clean. I, too, sulked in my own pity and humiliation. I was the mother, not Marisa. When you see Ally, please tell her that I love her and that I am really sorry."

"No problem."

Janice gives Janet a hug, and Janet holds on tightly, as if she is picturing the way she would want to hug Marisa if she had the opportunity one last time. Janet then gives a brave smile while letting go slowly. Janice holds back her tears and walks out of the apartment swiftly to stay strong. She can only imagine if her mother had to find out she died and could not be there for her child's last moments on earth.

The next day Janice goes to the group home to meet Ally and let her know the plan—Janice has to adopt Ally—as well as tell her about the winnings and to let her know what Marisa's dying request was.

Janice is in the visiting room waiting for Ally, drinking a bottle of ice tea. Her hands are shaking as she contemplates what approach to take to connect with Ally since she has quite a bit of information that has to be shared in a fifteen-minute visit.

Ally, shocked to have a visitor, notices that it is Janice and runs over and gives her such a big hug. This makes it that much harder for Janice to tell her about Marisa.

Janice says, "Hey, Ally, how are you?"

"I'm good as I can be. Why is my sister not with you?"

"Well, that's what I'm here for."

"OK, so what is it?"

"Your sister had cancer and died, and she wrote you a letter."

Janice then hands the book of Marisa over to let Ally read a personal letter that Marisa wrote specifically to Ally.

Dear Ally,

I'm sorry that I'm dying. I'm sorry that I am too pathetic to be right in front of you to tell you. By the time you read this, I will already be dead. I want you to know that I love you, and I feel very selfish that I forced the courts to allow me to become emancipated while you were sent to foster care due to Mom's issue. I should have done better to stay in touch with you and your social worker. I hope you remember the Prayer of Jabez. "Oh that you would bless me indeed, and enlarge my territory, that your hand would be with me. That you would keep me from evil so that I may not cause pain." The key things happened, maybe not the way I wanted them to happen, but they did. God blessed me with winning the lottery. Janice will explain that to you. My territory was enlarged because he gave me a blessing that can be shared and a story to be told. Although I die alone, I know God never left me, and although you may feel that Mom and I left you, God never did. You caused no one pain, but I know I caused you much by not being there and sending a letter instead. I love you more than you will ever know, Ally.

Marisa

Janice looks into Ally's eyes and sees tears coming down, which then brings Janice to tears. As they both start crying, they both give one another a hug. After they calm each other down, Janice then explains what Marisa meant in the letter.

"Marisa won a lot of money, and she wanted to make sure we would set up a trust fund for you as well as have you live with me. So I'm going to get a lawyer and start that process. Your sister also wanted you to carry her ashes. We are going to spread them in four locations. These are all the places she wanted to go as soon as she won the lottery. Unfortunately, she also found out she had cancer, all in the same day. Her wishes are all in the book with that page she left specifically for you."

"OK, I would love to have an actual home. That will be great if you can adopt me. I know my sister meant well, and I can't wait to meet all of her friends that she wanted to do this trip with. Hopefully, this is a way for us to always keep her in our memory."

"Exactly Your sister had a fun side to her, and when you meet the girls and read what she wrote in this book, you'll be amazed by her sense of humor."

"OK, I'm looking forward to it." Ally has joyful look, knowing her sister meant well, although she knows her sister died with guilt knowing how Ally's life had been thus far.

Three Months Later

Things moved forward. Janice claimed the ticket on behalf of Ally, since Ally was not of legal age, and set up a trust fund that held half of the winnings, while the remaining winnings were split between the girls.

The girls decided to publish Marisa's story as this was another one of Marisa's dying requests. So they published a book about four girls' journey across the world. Marisa's notebook was typed by Janice and became an instant best seller.

Janice eventually received custody of Ally. The girls took the ashes of their great friend Marisa and spread them in places she had always dreamed of going: Paris, Italy, Amsterdam, and Japan. During the trip, the girls did the pranks written in the book to the best of their ability. The girls lived life the way Marisa envisioned it.

On the trip the girls realized the lessons that Marisa tried to leave behind, and that is not to always be scared, to just live, just go for whatever you want. They proceeded to live life, not only on this trip but forever.

Ally decided to go in her sister's footsteps and take time to write down her thoughts like her sister.

Sometimes in life, we don't always have the choice to pick the luck we want. Sometimes the luck can feel joyful, like winning the lottery. Sometimes the luck or lack thereof is having cancer. Sometimes our luck is being able to reflect on the moments that made us change, made us have faith, and made us believe in something bigger than ourselves.

The positive of winning the lottery can be having the ability to do exactly what you want whenever you want. It has the psychological benefit of making you feel more confident and secure as everything is right in your grasp; you don't feel the pressure of bills. The negatives of winning the lottery are dealing with people wanting handouts and receiving notoriety to where you may feel uncomfortable as you don't want the fame of winning, just the results. The negative is cancer: death can feel right around the corner.

Most cancer patients deal with pain and suffering. Losing their hair, weight just being flat out miserable, cancer can change your whole outlook on life, can easily depress you instead of enjoying the opportunities you may have.

The positive of cancer is being able to reflect on the things you did in life. It makes you take a step back and appreciate what you have. Cancer allows you to feel every human emotion possible. It allows you to forgive; it allows you to want to love and feel real love.

Marisa longed to have these feelings, and she realized she was looking in all the wrong places. She did not need the money; she had everything that meant something right in front of her. Money meant nothing when she had cancer for the simple fact that the one thing she wanted to buy was time.

Time does not have a price tag; neither do memories. Money can only help in that process, so live life like today can be your last. Live the way my sister wished she did.

Until next time,

Ally

Acknowledgments

I want to thank my support system. Without you all, I could not take the time to create these pieces of work.

I am grateful for the opportunities that are given to me by God, and once again, I am just a grateful vessel of his that can be used.

This book is dedicated to all those that continue to move forward in life with a positive spirit, no matter their dilemmas. We can all learn from one another. I hope this book keeps dialog going to build a bridge for compassion.

www.brintonwoodall.com

About the Autor

Brinton was born in the Bronx, New York and raised in the greater New York area. During his childhood years numerous educators voiced to Brinton that he was learning disabled and would not graduate from high school. Nonetheless, Brinton excelled triumphing a multitude of obstacles and graduated from high school in 2008. His education did not stop there. He enrolled at New England College, completing his degree in three years. Brinton received his Bachelor of Arts degree in Business Administration with a minor in Sociology in 2011.

With a passion for expressing his life through words in order to touch the lives of others, Brinton continues to pursue his dream of becoming an established writer. His debut book, The Dreamer: The Boy Who Caught 22 was released in January 2014. The literary inspiration unveils the passionate journey to success despite coming from an economically depressed environment that lacks opportunities and hope. Jarred, does not allow this to stop his dream to make his family proud and find what he defines as success. Unsure how he will reach this pinnacle, Jarred finds encouragement from his deceased grandfather who enters his dreams. It is this encouragement that allows Jarred to follow his heart and create a world through faith.

www.brintonwoodall.com